THE ADVENTURES OF THE SNEEKY SNEEKERS

The Tornado

Characters created by Mike Jaroch

Written by F. A. "Randy" Jaroch, J. Chipp Jaroch, and
Timothy D. Jaroch

Illustrated by Lois Axeman

ℚ CHILDRENS PRESS, CHICAGO

Dedicated to Stanley and Jayne, our parents, and to Marsha, for her inspiration

Library of Congress Cataloging in Publication Data

Jaroch, F   A   Randy.
  The adventures of the Sneeky Sneekers: The Tornado

  SUMMARY: Magical powers from mysteriously acquired
sneakers enable four brothers to halt a tornado.
  [1. Tornadoes—Fiction] I. Jaroch, J. Chipp,
joint author. II. Jaroch, Timothy D., joint author.
III. Axeman, Lois. IV. Title.
PZ7.J292Ad   [Fic]   77-4844
ISBN 0-516-03405-7

PART ONE

Even if you had seen it with your own two eyes, chances are you wouldn't have believed it. For what happened to four young boys on that magical day had never happened before and would probably never happen again.

The four boys were brothers. Mike, Chipp, Randy, and Rod. They did everything together.

The magical day began with the boys anxiously waiting for the mailman. This was a very special day. It was the first day of summer, June 21st, and also Mike's birthday. Mike was the oldest brother. When they spotted Mr. Sutter, the mailman, turning the corner, the boys jumped up. Their eyes grew wide with excitement. Mr. Sutter was carrying a large box.

"Good morning boys!" he called. "I seem to have a present here. Wouldn't be somebody's birthday, now, would it?"

Mike was quick to raise his hand. "Yes Mr. Sutter, mine."

"Well, happy birthday, Mike!" Mr. Sutter set the box down, winked and turned to leave. "Whoops, almost forgot," he pulled a letter from his mailbag. On the back of the envelope in big letters was written, "READ THIS LETTER FIRST."

"Now be sure you read this first before you open that box," Mr. Sutter said as he left.

Rod, the youngest brother, had picked up the box. He was shaking it to guess what was inside.

Chipp spoke up. "Sounds as though it
holds a lot of smaller boxes. Maybe the
parts to some sort of electronic toy."
Chipp was very smart. He was good at
thinking things out.

"I'll bet I know what it is!" grinned Randy. "I bet it's a box full of empty boxes!"

Mike shook his head. "You and your silly jokes. We'd better read the letter. Something tells me this is important."

Mike opened the letter and began reading out loud.

Dear Michael,

Happy Birthday! Inside the box you will find four presents. The blue one is for you, the green one is for Chipp, the red is Randy's and the yellow is Rod's. Each gift has a magical power of it's own. You must use your magical powers to help others. Because you are the oldest Michael, you are in charge. Be careful. I will be writing to you again, soon.

Rod shivered. "Wow, that's kind of spooky, and look, the letter doesn't even have a name on it."

"Hmmmm, this is indeed mysterious," Chipp added, rubbing his chin.

Mike knew who had sent the gifts. There was only one person in the whole world who called him Michael. He stuck the letter into his back pocket. "See, I told you guys this was important. Come on now, let's check it out."

Rod ripped the box open. Inside there were four boxes. "Here you go, Mike, you first." He tossed the blue box to Mike, who tore away the wrapping and removed the lid.

"What? It's just a pair of blue sneakers with the name 'Mike' on the side."

Randy was into the red box. "Yeah, I've got a pair, too. Red ones with my name on the side."

"Same here!" Rod shouted.

"Likewise," mumbled Chipp.

How could sneakers have magical powers? they all wondered.

Mike was puzzled. "I don't know what this is all about guys, but let's find out."

All four sat down and put on their new shoes. Moments later, they were walking around nervously waiting for something special to happen.

But nothing happened. Finally Rod said, "Aw, this must be some kind of joke somebody's playing on us."

"I fail to see the humor in this prank," declared Chipp. "On the other hand, do you realize that the shortest distance between Boston and Chicago is exactly 867 air miles. That the number of people living in Los Angeles last year was 2,809,813, and . . . ."

Mike, Randy, and Rod stared in amazement. Then they said, "what are you talking about?"

Chipp blinked. "It just came to me. It's as though I were overcome by some strange power."

"Power!" Mike screamed, "Power, that's it! It's your sneakers. They must give you a special brain power."

Rod grabbed Mike's arm. "Don't look now, but I think Randy's sneakers gave him the power to disappear!"

"Hello, down there!" It was Randy. "I'm up here with the squirrels!"

They looked up and there he was, standing on the highest branch of their big, old oak tree.

"You mean you're up there with the other nuts," Rod said with a laugh.

Mike scratched his head. "OK, I give up, how did you get up that high?"

"Who knows," Randy chuckled. "I thought I'd see how good these sneakers were for jumping. And when I jumped up, I just kept going."

Mike snapped his fingers. "Your sneakers must make you extra light."

"That's just great!" Randy called out. "But how do I get down?"

"Easy," Rod said "the same way we get our kites down."

With that, he walked over and grabbed the trunk of the tree and began shaking it. But much to his surprise, the giant oak, roots and all, started to come right up out of the ground.

Mike yelled. "Stop, Rod, Stop! Your sneakers must give you some kind of super strength."

"Help, help," cried Randy, dangling from the branch. "I can't hold on much longer!" Suddenly the branch snapped, but Randy just floated to the ground.

"Wow," said Mike, "super smartness, super lightness, and super strength! It's true, we've got magical powers with these sneakers on." Mike wondered what power his sneakers gave him. He tried to jump, but nothing special happened. Then he tried to push the big oak tree, but he couldn't move it at all.

"Think about math," said Chipp, "that's what you have the most trouble with in school."

Mike tried very hard. He thought and
thought. But soon he realized that his
sneakers didn't make him any smarter.
''Maybe something's wrong with my
pair,'' he said sadly.

Just then their mother stepped out onto the porch. "Boys, where did you get those new sneakers?" she asked.

"In a surprise package that came in the mail," they answered. Before the boys could start to tell her about the magical powers, she said, "You can tell me all about your surprise later. Better put your old shoes on now. I want you to help me in the garden."

When she had gone, Mike said to his brothers, "Let's not tell anyone about the special powers until we can figure out what's wrong with my sneakers."

PART TWO

That night, long after his brothers had gone to sleep, Mike was still awake. His thoughts were racing. What was this all about? What did the letter mean about helping others? And why didn't his sneakers have any magical powers?

Suddenly a distant noise crept into the room. He had heard the eerie sound before. It was the tornado-warning siren. It meant that one of the dark and treacherous storms had been spotted nearby. Mike remembered what the letter had said. Could he and his brothers do something about a tornado? It seemed so impossible . . . and yet.

He jumped up and quickly woke his brothers. "Get your sneakers on! There's a tornado coming. We've got to do something!"

Randy rubbed his eyes and yawned, "Couldn't we do it in the morning?"

"Come on, come on, there's no time to lose. Mom and dad will be up soon!"

One by one, they slipped into their sneakers. Mike was holding open the bedroom window.

"Down the oak tree," he whispered, "and hurry!"

Ever so quietly they slid across the roof onto the branches of the big tree. They inched their way down, all except Randy, who simply floated to the ground.

"OK Chipp," Mike said, once they all were safely on the ground. "You've got the super smartness, so think. Think hard. What should we do?"

Chipp rubbed his chin. "Well, it's a fact that tornados travel in a southwesterly to northeasterly direction. I think that our first course of action would be to have Randy jump as high as he can and check out the sky toward the southwest. He can give us an eyewitness report on the storm."

Mike tapped Randy on the back. "OK Randy, up you go."

Randy took a deep breath. "Ready for takeoff!" With the slightest jump he went up, up, up. High above the rooftops, he hovered for a few moments.

Then he floated down, down, down.

"Whee, this is fun!"

"Come on, keep your mind on what we sent you up there for!"

"Oh yeah, I'm sorry. Well, there are dark clouds and lightning out by the farms south of town. Looks like it could hit pretty soon."

"Right. OK, guys," said Mike, "get your bikes and follow me." They all ran to the garage to get their bikes, but Mike zoomed there in a flash. When the others finally got to the garage, they all knew what magical power Mike's sneakers gave him. "I've got super speed," he said excitedly.

Like a race car, Mike shot away into the night. Chipp, Randy, and Rod jumped on their bikes and pedaled after him. Just south of town, Mike screeched to a halt on Route 1, an old farm road. He could see that all the farm families had their house lights on. They were already taking safety precautions against the storm. But there were no lights on at Farmer Gray's house.

"Oh, oh," he told himself, "that's right. Farmer Gray can't hear too well. Gosh, he probably doesn't even know the tornado is coming!"

Mike ran again, faster, faster, and faster down the road and right up to Farmer Gray's door. As hard as he could, he banged and banged on the door. But nothing happened. He ran to the back door and banged on that. But still no one answered. And all the while, the wind was growing stronger, the clouds darker and more dangerous. He was glad to see his three brothers.

"Rod, Rod!" Mike shouted through the howling wind. "Everyone has gone to safety but Farmer Gray. He can't hear me knocking."

Rod jumped off his bike and ran to the corner of the tall old house. "The best way to wake someone up is to shake them a little." With almost no effort at all Rod lifted the corner of the house right off the ground and shook it. Carefully placing the house back on its foundation, he ran back to his brothers.

Lights flashed on, and moments later the front door flew open. Farmer Gray, with his calico cat under his arm, ran into the yard. "Holy cow, Ezmeralda. Did you feel this old house a shakin? We better get ourselves down to the storm shelter, quick! Looks like a bad one comin'!"

"Rod, you're probably the world's first human alarm clock," Mike said. "Good job."

"Right!" Randy added. "Now there's just one more thing we have to do."

"What's that?" they all asked.

Randy pointed to the sky. "Run!"

There it was, coming right at them, a swirling, twisting funnel of a tornado.

Chipp stopped them. "Wait," he said.
"It occurs to me that the easiest way to
stop a tornado is to create a force moving
in the opposite direction of the funnel."

Mike quickly went into action. He
began running in a wide circle around the
tornado. Faster, faster, faster he ran,
until he became no more than a blurr.

Chipp shouted, "Look! Mike's speed is slowing down the tornado!"

"The funnel cloud is getting smaller!" yelled Randy.

"It's disappearing!" Rod screamed.

Suddenly the wind stopped. The danger was over. Mike's human tornado had been too powerful. Slowly, Mike came into sight. He finally came to a stop. "Whew! Let's go home guys. I think we've done enough good for one night."

PART THREE

Back home, they talked about their first adventure.

"Boy, wait till I tell the kids at school!" Randy laughed. "They'll never believe me."

"I don't think it's wise to say anything to anyone," Chipp said.

"Right," added Mike. "No one should know about our powers, ever! Is that clear?"

Randy giggled. "I guess you're right. I guess we'll have to be sneaky about our sneakers."

Mike sat up in bed. "Hey, that's no joke." That's a good name for us. Let's even be sneaky about how we spell it. THE SNEEKY SNEEKERS. Our own secret club. What do you think, guys?"

They all agreed. "THE SNEEKY SNEEKERS it is!"

The next morning at breakfast, the boys ate quietly while their father read the newspaper.

"We certainly were lucky last night, boys. Seems a real bad twister was headed this way. Some folks saw it start to come down by Old Farmer Gray's place. But then it just disappeared, didn't do any damage at all. We were all pretty lucky, I'd say."

From behind his paper he couldn't see the boys smile and wink at each other.

"Yes, Dad," answered Mike, "and I have the feeling that it's just the beginning of a lot of good luck."

About the Creator

Mike Jaroch is presently a personnel manager for a hospital supply company in Round Lake, Illinois. He lives with his wife Marsha and their two children, Julie and Michael, in Lake Villa, Illinois.

The idea for the Sneeky Sneekers adventures came from Mike's own experiences. Years ago Mike organized a similar club with his brothers, Chipp, Randy, and Rod. As members of a large family [13 children and 2 adults], the club provided the four boys with a wonderful outlet for their childhood fantasies.

About the Authors

F. A. "Randy" Jaroch, a free-lance advertising copywriter, lives in Omaha, Nebraska with his wife Jeanne and their two children. A published poet, Randy also edits a weekly poetry column for the Omaha *World-Herald*.

J. Chipp Jaroch is a programmer analyst for a community college in northern Illinois. He lives in a rambling old farmhouse near Ingleside, Illinois.

Timothy D. Jaroch is an attorney-at-law for a large law firm in Boston, Massachusetts. He and his wife Patti and their four sons live in Belmont, Massachusetts.

About the Artist

Lois Axeman is a native Chicagoan who lives with her husband and two children in the city. After attending the American Academy and the Institute of Design (IIT), Lois started as a fashion illustrator in a department store. When the children's wear illustrator became ill, Lois took her place and found she loved drawing children. She started free-lancing then, and has been doing text and picture books ever since.